How the Rhinoceros got his Skin

Miles Kelly

Once upon a time, on a lonely island
on the shores of the Red Sea,
there lived a man.

He owned nothing in the world
but his hat and his knife and a
cooking stove (of the kind that
you must particularly
never touch).

The man was very happy.
He had nothing to worry him.

Except...

...one rhinoceros, who lived in the very middle of the island.

He had a horn on his nose and two piggy eyes.

Hrumph!

In those days the rhinoceros's skin fitted him quite tight. There were no wrinkles in it anywhere.

He had no manners then, and he has no manners now, and he never will have any manners.

One day the man took flour and water and currants and plums and sugar and other delicious things, and made himself one big cake.

It was two feet across and three feet thick.

He put it on the
stove, and he baked
it and he baked it
till it was all
beautifully brown.

It smelled YUMMY!

The rhinoceros smelled the delicious smell.
Just as the man was going to eat his cake,
along it came.

In two shakes of a tail,
the man climbed to the top
of a tall palm tree and hid.

The rhinoceros upset the stove with his nose, and the cake rolled onto the sand.

Then the rhinoceros went away
waving his tail, back to his home
in the very middle of the island.

The man came down from his palm tree and cleaned up the mess. As he cleaned, he thought of a plan, and he sang to himself,

"Them that takes cakes
Which the man bakes
Makes dreadful mistakes!"

A few weeks later, there was a heat wave in the Red Sea. It was so hot that everybody took off their clothes. The man even took off his hat!

In those days the rhinoceros's skin buttoned underneath with three buttons.

The rhinoceros took off his skin to have a **cooling swim** in the sea.

The rhinoceros did not say sorry to the
man for eating his cake – he had no manners
then, and he has no manners now...

and he never will
have any manners.

Splash!

He waddled straight into
the water and blew bubbles
through his nose, leaving
his skin on the beach.

But the man found the skin, and he
smiled a big smile. Then he danced
three times round the skin and
rubbed his hands.

The man filled his hat with crumbs. He had plenty, because he never ate anything but cake, and he never swept out his camp.

Then he took that skin,
and he shook that skin,
and he scrubbed that skin,
and he rubbed that skin.

At last it was as full of
dry, stale, tickly
cake crumbs (and some
burned currants) as it
could possibly be.

Then the man climbed to the
top of his palm tree and waited.

When the rhinoceros came in from his swim, he put on his skin and buttoned it up with the three buttons.

And it tickled just like cake crumbs in bed.

Then he wanted to scratch, but that made it worse!

Then he lay down on the sands and
rolled and rolled...

Then he ran to the palm tree and rubbed and rubbed and rubbed himself against it.

He rubbed a wrinkle over his shoulders, and another underneath, and more on his legs.

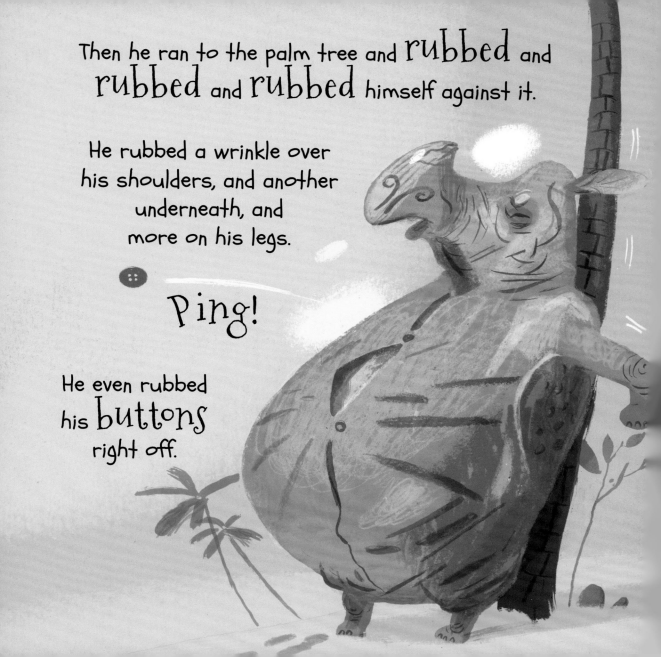

Ping!

He even rubbed his buttons right off.

It spoiled his temper, but it didn't make any difference to the crumbs. So he went home, very angry and horribly scratchy.

The man came down from his palm tree, and felt quite pleased with himself.

From that day to this, every rhinoceros has great folds in his skin and a **very bad temper,** all because of the cake crumbs inside.

Grrummph!